Happy Springtime!

Kate McMullan

PICTURES BY
Sujean Rim

NEAL PORTER BOOKS
HOLIDAY HOUSE / NEW YORK

Neal Porter Books

HOLIDAY HOUSE is registered in the U.S. Patent and Trademark Office.

Printed and bound in November 2020 at Leo Paper, Heshan, China.

The artwork for this book was created using watercolor, pencil, crayon, and collage.

Book design by Jennifer Browne

www.holidayhouse.com

First Edition

10   9   8   7   6   5   4   3   2   1

Library of Congress Cataloging-in-Publication Data

Names: McMullan, Kate, author. | Rim, Sujean, illustrator.

Title: Happy springtime! / by Kate McMullan ; illustrated by Sujean Rim.

Description: First edition. | New York : Holiday House, [2020] | "A Neal

Porter book." | Audience: Ages 4 to 8 | Audience: Grades K–1 | Summary:

"A celebration and explanation of the Spring Equinox"— Provided by publisher.

Identifiers: LCCN 2020017021 | ISBN 9780823445516 (hardcover)

Subjects: LCSH: Spring—Juvenile literature. | Vernal equinox—Juvenile literature.

Classification: LCC QB637.5 .M42 2020 | DDC 508.2—dc23

LC record available at https://lccn.loc.gov/2020017021

ISBN 978-0-8234-4551-6 (hardcover)

For Arthur and Lily —K.M.

To this wonderful world —S.R.

HERE'S A MESSAGE

for school bus riders
heading out on a cold, dark morning,

for red-breasted birds
pecking at ice-coated berries,

for all those whose snowsuits have stuck zippers,

and those with their boots on the wrong feet,

for crossing guards wearing earmuffs
and two pairs of mittens,
for dogs dressed in
sweaters and booties—

DO NOT LOSE HEART!

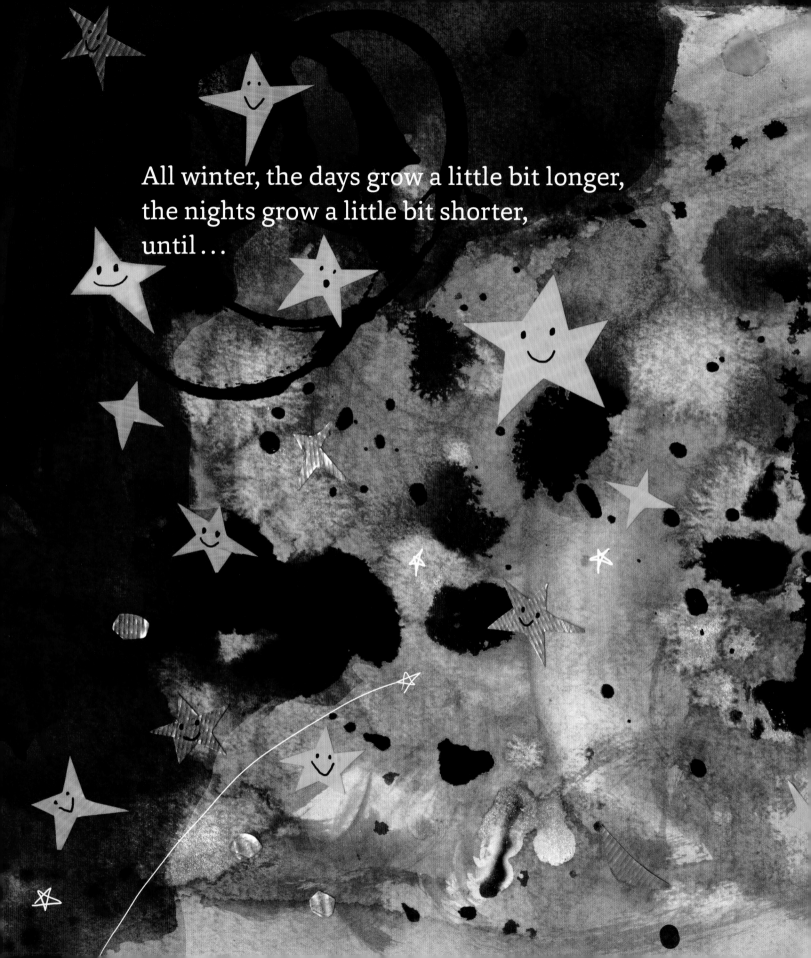

All winter, the days grow a little bit longer,
the nights grow a little bit shorter,
until . . .

the day becomes exactly
as long as the night.

On this day
we say . . .

HAPPY SPRINGTIME!

To bouncers of balls and sliders on slides,

to sandbox diggers and swingers on swings,

to groggy frogs waking from their winter's sleep,
to trees unfurling their leaves in the light.

The days are
growing longer!

Happy springtime
to smock-wearing painters of flowers and bugs,

to green shoots and pink worms
poking up from the soil,

to winter-born babies
who've not seen a spring,

to black-capped birds
plucking moss for their nests.

Celebrate the sun
you wielders of
watering cans,

you riders
of bicycles,

you runners passing
sweet-smelling fields
of new grass,

you turtles basking
on warm rocks,

you young raccoons
napping on sunlit branches.

The days are growing longer!

Rejoice in the rain
you walkers with
colorful umbrellas,
you puddle jumpers,

you small brown birds
splashing on sidewalks,
you lovers of mud.

Listen for spring
in the crack of a bat hitting a ball,
in the opening creak of a long-closed window,

in the gurgle of icy streams melting,
in the buzz of bees burrowing in blossoms.

The days are growing longer!

Count spring

in ducklings swimming
after their mamas,

1

2

3

4

in grimy vehicles waiting at the car wash,

in butterflies flitting among the lilacs,

in muddy boots lined up outside the door.

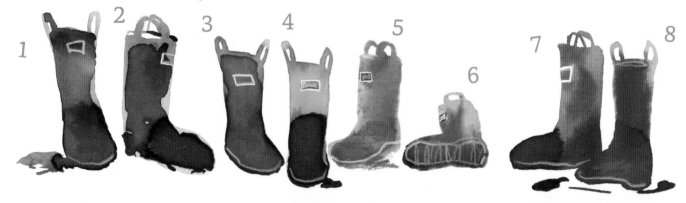

Sing to the spring
you peepers in ponds,

you songsters in music class,

you bright red birds
calling your mates,
you skippers of ropes
chanting your rhymes.

The days are growing
longer and longer
and longer
until …
we reach the longest
day of the year.

On this day we say …